TILLY AND ELMER
COLLECTED STORIES

The Sexy Seniors of South Branch

GENE CLEMENTS

Pickleworks Press

Acknowledgments:

This book came about largely because of the encouragement of many people, most of whom didn't know they were encouraging me, and probably have wished they had not done so, now that they know I keep bringing Tilly and Elmer up in every conversation.

Many of these folks are part of the little group of coffee drinkers, known to some as the "Dull Men's Club", who gather most mornings to discuss the state of the world, to exaggerate the passionate exploits they experienced in high school fifty years ago, and to impress one another with their knowledge of carburetors.

I'm especially grateful to Ann who has encouraged me, even when she knew where her encouragement was leading, and who seems to be almost as fond of Tilly and Elmer as I am.

A profound "Thank You!" also goes to my editor, Elizabeth Johnson, who must have realized the magnitude of the task ahead when she found that the very first word, beyond the title page, was misspelled.

~ ~ ~

ISBN-10: 0-99628270-X
ISBN-13: 978-0-9962827-0-3

Pickleworks Press

CONTENTS

Introduction

Prologue

1 Skinny-Dipping Scandal   1

2 50th Class Reunion   19

3 Tilly and Elmer Go to Las Vegas   33

4 Tilly and Elmer Get Crazy   49

5 Truck Tryst   61

6 Tilly and Elmer Get Warmed Up   73

7 Tilly's Afternoon Delight   85

About the Author   99

Additional Titles   101

INTRODUCTION

These fictional stories chronicle the humorous, romantic, and often erotic adventures of Tilly and Elmer, a Midwestern couple in their late sixties. They've been married for close to fifty years, they still really like each other, and they know what to do about it.

Tilly and Elmer would appear to the casual observer to be the definition of an "old married couple". But while they ARE a couple, AND married, they don't consider themselves OLD. In fact, they still feel like teenagers most of the time, although sometimes events remind them that they aren't quite as athletic, skinny, or flexible, as they were five decades ago. No matter. They try to recapture their youth anyway; and when they can't quite recapture it, they at least give it a good chase. Along the way, they have some fun and get themselves into, and usually out of, some humorous situations. What they've lost over the years in body tone, they have gained in expertise, imagination, and good humor. Tilly and Elmer would never want to shock anyone, but what could be more shocking than an erotic story where the protagonists are shocked when they hear others use profanity?

Tilly and Elmer live on a small farm near the made up town of South Branch, Iowa. They were high school sweethearts and have lived in South Branch all their lives, except, of course, during the four years in the mid 1960's when Elmer was in college in Cedar Falls and Tilly was studying nursing (among other things) in San Francisco.

That's another story, but so far, Tilly hasn't been too keen on letting me write it.

PROLOGUE

"I saw the cutest top over at Madeline's just now. It's a little bit expensive, but I think it would look good with the black skirt I wear when we go out for dinner sometimes. It's low cut, the way you like, and I could wear the necklace with the little heart on it that dangles down into my cleavage. The top is a lovely dark blue with stripes. Do you think I should get it?"

"I love stripes!" Elmer said.

His gaze was focused out the window of Pearl's Downtown Diner. A half-finished bowl of ice cream on the table in front of him was melting in the soggy heat of a summer afternoon in South Branch.

"So you think I should get it then?"

"Get what?"

"The striped top I just told you about! What's so interesting out there?" she said, turning to follow Elmer's gaze, which led to a striped skirt wrapped tightly around the hips of what appeared to be a girl of eighteen or so.

The girl was chatting flirtatiously with a handsome young man who was leaning against a car. The striped skirt that Elmer found so interesting was breathtakingly short, and from time to time the young lady would surreptitiously tug on it in a failed attempt to make it slightly longer.

"Come on Elmer. She's a half century younger than you are, I doubt she will be rolling in the hay with you anytime soon."

"Well, she does look very attractive in that skirt and that halter top, but this time I wasn't imagining rolling in the hay with her."

"Of course not. You would never think such a thing," Tilly chuckled. "What **were** you thinking, then?"

"I'd rather not say."

"I've known you for fifty years Elmer."

"All right. I hate to admit this, but I was wondering if we were in high school with her grandmother."

"I'll bet her grandmother would have something to say about that outfit!" said Tilly. "We girls didn't dress that way when you and I were that age!"

"Well, even so, you always got my attention. And even then I got especially turned on when you were wearing stripes."

"Elmer?"

"What?"

"Finish your ice cream and let's head for home."

"Why?"

"Because under this dress, I'm wearing striped panties."

~~~
~~~

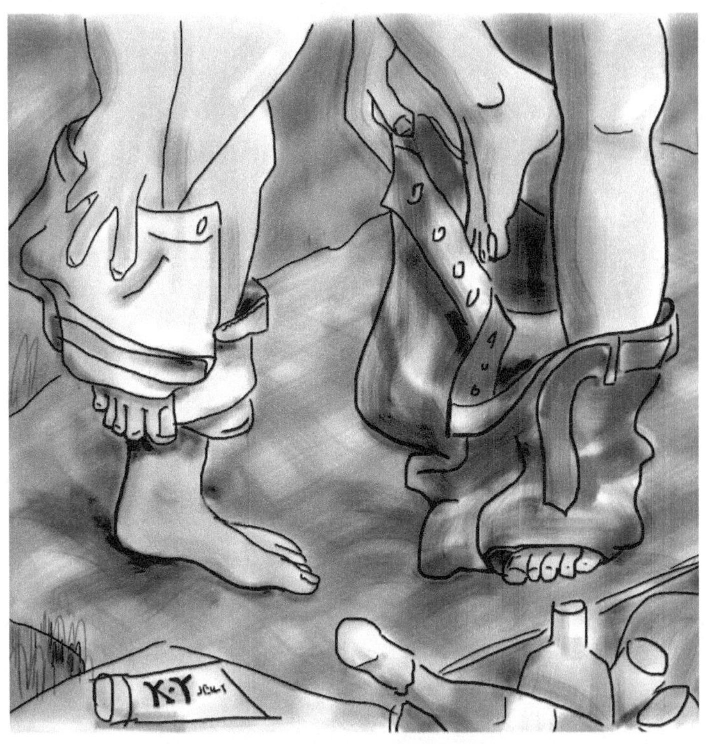

SKINNY-DIPPING SCANDAL

"Wake up Elmer! It's a spectacular summer Saturday outside!" called Tilly from the kitchen.

Elmer could smell the coffee and a glance out the window confirmed Tilly's assertion. Elmer wandered into the kitchen, still in his underwear. Tilly put her arms around him and gave him a long romantic kiss. "What's gotten into you?" he asked.

"Nothing so far," she said, rubbing her hand over the front of his boxers. "But I hope that will change pretty soon. Doesn't this kind of day make you feel eighteen again?"

"Yes, and so does that kind of greeting," replied Elmer, feeling the fabric of his boxers tightening.

"Want to make love to me all day?" asked Tilly.

"Can we have breakfast first?"

"Yes, I want you to be at full strength and we might forget to eat the food we're taking on our picnic."

"So we're going on a sexy 'picnic,' are we? Maybe we can eat in between times, just like we used to," laughed Elmer. "Where do you have in mind for this outing?"

"Down by the creek near the big oak tree, our old favorite spot," replied Tilly.

"Good idea. I'll go find the swimming suits," said Elmer, starting toward the bedroom.

Tilly gently took his hand and said conspiratorially, "We won't be needing any swimming suits today, Elmer. We went swimming without them at eighteen and I feel eighteen this morning."

"But what if someone else shows up while we're down there skinny-dipping?"

"Nobody is going to show up, and if they do, we'll quickly get our clothes on before they catch sight of us," Tilly giggled. "Besides, as you used to say fifty years ago, Elmer, 'If they haven't seen it before, they won't know what it is anyway!' "

After breakfast, they packed a picnic basket with all the fancy food they could find in the cupboard.

"Shall I bring the bottle of Champagne we've been saving for a special occasion?" asked Elmer.

"No question about it," enthused Tilly. "I'm expecting this to be the most special occasion of the weekend!"

After a ten minute walk through the woods, they reached their favorite spot, a small clearing next to the creek, on the bank nearest their house. The clearing opened on a part of the creek that widened out to make a four-foot-deep pool of slow moving water with a sandy bank. A large oak tree, whose lower foliage touched the surface of the pool, afforded a shady hideaway at one side of the clearing. A smaller clearing across the forty-foot-wide pool was accessible, for anyone knowing about it, by walking along the edge of the neighbor's field, but very few people knew about it, and anyone approaching would be visible in time to allow for a quick cover up

The day was reminiscent of the summer days they had spent together as teenagers, and, except for the occasional reminder caused by an aching knee or clumsy step, they might as well have been eighteen again. They laid the blanket on the soft grass under the oak tree and stashed the picnic basket in the shade. Laughing like adolescents, they got undressed in the clearing, throwing their clothes over the trunk of a downed tree. The warm sun felt delicious on their bare skin, and the vaguely sexy smell of summer in the Midwest filled the air. They were sweating from their walk, and the cool water felt refreshing as they carefully waded into the pool. Before long they were having a wonderful time splashing and teasing each other, taking time out now and then for a romantic embrace.

Their watery foreplay, however, masked the sounds of someone approaching the clearing across the creek. By the time they heard voices, the interlopers were about to reach the opposite clearing where Elmer and Tilly would be fully visible in all their glory. There was no time to retrieve their clothes so they ducked under the overhanging branches of the oak tree, their bodies submerged with only their heads above water, hidden by the foliage. They dared not climb up on the bank lest they be seen. They looked at each other, suppressing giggles at their predicament.

A couple came into view in the small clearing, no farther away than their garden was from the house. A giggling young woman was thrown over a young man's shoulder, his right arm around her thighs with her kicking lower legs extending in front of him. In his left hand, he carried a six-pack of beer and under his arm, a blanket and a box of donuts. Apparently they were also intent on an afternoon picnic. Tilly and Elmer were able to find an underwater seat on one of the submerged oak roots and settled down to wait for the visitors to leave.

"Oh, my god!" Elmer whispered to Tilly.
"Right, I hope they don't notice our clothes draped

over that log on this side of the creek," responded Tilly.

"Not only that, I recognize that girl. It's Molly, the young woman who waits tables at Pearl's Diner every morning when my friends and I go there for coffee!"

Tilly playfully poked Elmer in the ribs. The young couple spread out their blanket, shed their clothing, enthusiastically applied sunscreen to each other, and were soon running stark naked toward the water, leaping into the pool with a double splash.

Molly and her friend frolicked in the water, alternately engaging in affection and horseplay. The latter involved the young man lifting his partner out of the water and tossing her into the air, and Molly trying the same with her boyfriend, with less success. After some time at this, on one toss she landed on a submerged log, letting out a squeal. Molly limped out of the water and sat down on the blanket.

The young man examined a red spot on her thigh and said, "You're going to have a bruise there tomorrow, Baby. Maybe a kiss will make it all better."

He kissed the spot sand they heard Molly say, "Oh! That does feel better, but there's another spot that needs the same treatment."

She spread her legs apart to indicate the location

she had in mind as her young man eagerly began the required therapy.

"I can't watch this!" whispered Elmer.

"You can close your eyes if you want to," Tilly responded, "but I'm hoping to acquire some new ideas."

"OK," said Elmer. "But only in the interest of education."

"Right," smiled Tilly.

Watching the young couple WAS educational in its way. Tilly and Elmer were amazed by the graceful movements of the young lovers; they seemed to be able to effortlessly lift and bend their bodies into any position they wished. It was a good thing, because, in the span of five minutes, they tried every position Tilly and Elmer had ever thought of. It was like a dance where the artists seemed to think that each position was inferior to the one they planned to try next. Before long however, the young man found a position that was to his liking and the dance was quickly over. This was followed by a whispered conversation that Tilly and Elmer couldn't hear. Molly and her friend opened two of the beers and the box of donuts, interrupting their lunch frequently for a bit of wrestling. By the time their repast was over, each had downed two cans of Bud Lite. The young man opened one of the final, now warm, cans of beer and playfully poured it over Molly's chest. She retaliated by shaking her last can, popping it open, and chasing the young man across the clearing, spraying him unmercifully.

"At least they finally discovered the best use for Bud Lite," Elmer whispered. "I don't think they will hang out here much longer."

Apparently, Elmer had forgotten one of the benefits of being eighteen years old. After a quick rinse in the pool, the dancers began another performance, similar to the first in that they couldn't quite seem to find the perfect blending of their respective anatomies. This one lasted a bit longer however, and in the end, clearly met with Molly's approval. Once finished, they unhurriedly got dressed, collected their gear, and disappeared up the path.

Tilly and Elmer slowly arose from their underwater seats and awkwardly exited the water.

Elmer groaned. "It's a good thing they were young folks. If it had taken them any longer, I'd be fossilized by now."

"Don't give me an opening line like that, Elmer," Tilly laughed. "Come on old man, forget those amateurs and show me how an expert does it."

Tilly lay down on the blanket, rolled onto her side carefully, and extracted a tube of KY Jelly from the picnic basket. She applied it liberally as Elmer stood next to her, contemplating the best way to ease himself down to his customary position. He bent over from the waist, putting his hands on his knees, then moved his left foot back, bending his knees and clumsily planting his left hand and left knee to the ground next to Tilly.

Elmer turned his upper body to face her, extended his right arm across her chest, and placed his right hand on the ground next to her left breast. Once he had regained his balance, he swung his right leg over her, and, ignoring a twinge in his lower back, lowered himself a little awkwardly onto her. Tilly wrapped her arms around him and eased him into position, guiding his body into a perfect fit with hers.

"There's no substitute for experience, big boy," she murmured, squeezing him tight.

They made love slowly and gently, in no hurry to be finished, changing positions slightly now and then when one or the other felt a cramp coming on. Each knew instinctively when the other was about to reach a climax, and for some time they took turns easing up on their ministrations to maddeningly prolong each other's pleasure. Eventually they both knew without any outward communication that this game had gone on as long as necessary, and first Tilly, then Elmer reached a quiet but convulsive culmination to the afternoon's main event. For some time afterward, they held each other as they regained their bearings. When a conversation began, they complimented each other's performance and wondered aloud why they didn't spend every afternoon that way.

They eventually realized they were hungry and moved on to the dining portion of the picnic. It was late in the afternoon by the time they finished the bottle of Champagne and began packing up for the walk home. It had been the sweetest summer afternoon they had spent in a long time. As they reluctantly got dressed, Elmer remembered the entertainment from the beginning of their sojourn by the creek.

"I hope I don't start blushing Monday morning when Molly brings us our coffee," he mused.

Tilly regarded him with a smile. "Now I can see why you go down there every morning! I didn't think a bunch of old geezers were the only attraction at Pearl's, and Molly IS adorable. Of course, she's young enough to be your granddaughter."

"Thanks for pointing that out," groaned Elmer.

When Elmer met his buddies at the "geezers' table" at Pearl's Diner on Monday morning, he paid even closer attention than usual to Molly. When she came to their table with a fresh pot of coffee, Elmer put on his most fatherly face and asked about the obvious bruise on her leg.

"Oh that? My boyfriend Randy and me were down at the creek fooling around on Saturday and I hit my leg on a log when he tossed me into the water."

"Ouch!" said Elmer, sympathetically.

"Didn't you see us?" asked Molly, quizzically.

"See you?" said Elmer, feigning innocence. He took a drink of coffee in hopes someone would begin a new topic.

"Well, we saw your clothes on the log and you and Mrs. Talbot under the big tree, so we thought you must have been watching us," Molly said casually.

Elmer gasped, inhaling a bit of coffee, which caused a coughing fit that turned his face beet red. Tears streamed down his face. This had the benefit of giving him a minute to think, although the extra minute didn't result in any clever response.

"I hope you're not upset," said Molly. "Me and Randy thought it was fun that you and Mrs. Talbot were watching us do it."

"You thought it was fun?" choked Elmer.

"Sure. And kind of kinky."

"I'm sorry," Elmer stammered.

Molly couldn't figure out why Mr. Talbot would be sorry she and Randy were having fun. Nevertheless, he still seemed a little upset for some reason. She looked at Elmer and smiled the sort of kindhearted smile that a teenager uses when addressing a hopelessly ancient person.

"We were really surprised to see you and Mrs. Talbot fucking on the bank when we came back down to look for Randy's lost phone. We didn't think old people…, I mean elderly…, I mean, um, senior citizens ever did that."

Elmer's face went from red to ghostly white. He folded his arms on the table in front of him and buried his head in them.

"Gosh, Mr. Talbot, didn't you want us to watch you? Since you were right across the creek and that old tree didn't hide you very well, we thought you liked knowing we were watching. Especially since we weren't hiding or anything."

Elmer's friends were enjoying the conversation, but Molly could see that Elmer was not, and tried again, a little louder in case he was hard of hearing. "It was very sweet how gentle and loving you and Mrs. Talbot were with each other."

No response from Elmer.

"You didn't even squash her when you got on top!"

Again, Elmer didn't respond.

"And it was awesome how long you were able to

keep it up! Randy can't fuck me for more than five minutes before he's squirting a gallon of come all over the place. I told him on the way home I hoped me and him, I mean him and me, would be like you guys when we got old."

Curiously, even this compliment didn't seem to raise Elmer's spirits. Molly figured it was an old person thing that she couldn't understand. Or else Mr. Talbot had dozed off like her grandfather sometimes did at dinner.

"Would anyone like more coffee?" she inquired, brightly.

Elmer slowly sat up and looked at her. Speaking softly, he said, "Molly, would you mind keeping this news just among us here at the table? I don't want everyone in town talking about it."

"OK," Molly agreed. "I'll stop tweeting about it. But I don't know if you can get rid of a youtube video once it's been posted."

Postscript:

When Elmer got home from Pearl's and told Tilly what had transpired at the diner, she was furious. Elmer had rarely seen Tilly so angry. She denounced people who had no respect for common decency. She railed against decadence. She pilloried the kind of person who would slander others without regard for the consequences. "People like that should go to jail!" she ranted.

Elmer tried his best to defend Molly.

"She wasn't being disrespectful," he said. "Young people just take sex for granted, and with all the social media stuff around they share things that were private back in our day."

"Elmer! I'm not talking about MOLLY!"

"You're not? ... Are you mad at ME then?" asked Elmer, warily.

"NO, DAMMIT, I'M MAD AT GENE, THAT JERK!"

"Oh! Well...," said Elmer. "I don't like everything he writes about us either, but come on Tilly, he has been pretty kind to us in general."

"You call that rubbish 'KIND?' And another thing! I don't like how excited he gets when he's drawing me naked!"

"I understand Tilly, but look at it this way. With a touch of a stylus on his iPad, he could give you fifty extra pounds and make my buns saggy. And, with a few keystrokes he could get us into real trouble. What if our author was somebody like Tennessee Williams? You could be an alcoholic, making out with an iguana in the back of a streetcar, or something."

Tilly began to calm down a little. "Well, I guess you're right," she said "He does let us have very nice sex most of the time."

"Right, I don't think we should make him mad or anything."

"OK," said Tilly. "But if he keeps writing that kind of stuff, I might call up that woman who just won the Nobel Prize and see if she needs any new characters!"

"Alice Munro you mean?"

Yes!" she said.

"Tilly, perhaps you should read some of her short stories before you try to talk her into writing about us," advised Elmer.

~~~
~~~

TILLY AND ELMER'S
50TH CLASS REUNION

"Here it is, Elmer! The news we've been waiting for!" announced Tilly excitedly, waving her iPad in the air.

"Is there a new drug that will make us eighteen

again?" asked Elmer. "That would be just in the nick of time!"

"Almost that good, it's the date of our fiftieth high school class reunion!"

"Oh. I was hoping for the fountain of youth in pill form," Elmer said glumly.

Tilly had been excited for months about their upcoming fiftieth high school class reunion. Elmer had been dreading it for the same length of time. Tilly and Elmer's differing feelings about the reunion had the same cause: "Buff" Stevens. Tilly had dated Buff for a while. Of course what girl hadn't? But Elmer liked her too and didn't feel he had a chance with her as long as Buff was in the picture. Buff was strikingly handsome, the quarterback of the football team, and the most popular boy in school. Elmer wasn't. Elmer consoled himself with the idea that he was smarter and funnier than Buff, which was true, but that seemed little consolation. It was only after Buff took up with the head cheerleader that Tilly had discovered her friend Elmer had some agreeable qualities.

Tilly knew Elmer was apprehensive about Buff, and was a bit flattered by it. A whiff of jealously on Elmer's part could liven up their sex life and might even convince him to do the dishes now and then. Of course, she hoped Buff would, at least, express a tiny moment of regret that he had let her get away, but she had gotten over Buff long ago. Nevertheless, she wasn't above having some fun teasing Elmer about the situation.

"Elmer, do you think I should wear this red dress, or this black one?" Tilly asked one morning.

"Are you going to a party or something?" inquired Elmer, puzzled.

"I mean to the reunion, silly."

"Tilly, the reunion is still a month away!" Elmer reminded her.

"You're right!" she mused. "I still have time to buy a new one! What color do you think Buff would like best?"

Elmer, for his part, tried not to think about the reunion. He had no desire to see Buff again, and the more he thought about it, that attitude extended to quite a few of his former classmates. He was undecided, though, about whether he wanted to see Susan Bell. He had had a huge crush on his "Suziebelle" in high school. They had been friends, but Elmer had been intimidated by the fact that she was, in his opinion, the cutest girl in the universe. Even after fifty years he could perfectly visualize his Suziebelle at seventeen; the curly black hair, the angelic smile, the beautiful shape of her breasts, and the luscious sound of her voice. He had spent the best part of three years fantasizing in exquisite detail how he would drive her wild with passion in the back seat of his dad's Ford sedan. Of course it was hopeless. She was so cute he assumed she had boyfriends lined up taking numbers at her door and that he would stand no chance of getting a date with her. Elmer was naturally curious about what had happened to Suziebelle, but to his chagrin he realized that if she were at the reunion, he'd probably become, momentarily at least, the same tongue-tied adolescent he had been when he last saw her.

"Suziebelle probably won't be there anyway, and if she is, we probably won't even recognize each other," thought Elmer.

Tilly remembered their classmate of course, and she

knew Elmer had been infatuated with Susan before they started dating. But Elmer had never pointed out to Tilly that all the romantic moves he practiced on her in his old Chevy pickup fifty years ago had originally been conceived as he was fantasizing about treating Suziebelle to his carnal creativity in the back seat of his old man's Ford.

The evening of the reunion finally arrived, and, in view of the occasion, they decided to make their entrance driving the same 1952 Chevy pickup, now lovingly restored. Tilly looked great in her new dress, which both delighted and worried Elmer, and by the time they arrived at the South Branch High School gym he was in a grumpy mood. When they got there, the gym was already filled with old people. For a moment, Elmer thought they were the old faculty, but, distressingly, they were his former classmates. His mood descended even further.

Tilly immediately fell into a conversation with one of her old girlfriends while Elmer made his way to the bar. When he brought Tilly her gin and tonic she thanked him with a pat on the arm, then headed off in the direction of a cluster of giggling women. Elmer took up a position in an opposite corner, hoping to watch the proceedings without having to actually interact with anybody. He tried to blend into the woodwork as he sipped his drink, glancing from time to time in the direction of the flock of women surrounding someone he assumed was Buff Stevens.

"Hi handsome!"

Elmer became aware of a soft, familiar voice as he felt a gentle touch on his shoulder. He turned around.

"Suziebelle!" he blurted, thus making his first faux pas of the evening. Susan had never heard him call her "Suziebelle"; he only used his pet name for her in his fantasies.

"Well, it's not Susan BELL any more," she said, smiling, "but I'm flattered you remember me."

"I couldn't, um, not forget to ahh, remember you, Susan!"

She still had the same curls and angelic smile. The curves were a little less perky, but she was still as cute as ever. Elmer became seventeen again.

They pulled out two chairs from one of the large round tables that were set for dinner and turned them to face each other. The conversation began with a quick recap of the last half century. Susan had been married after college, moved to the East Coast, and had two girls who were now grown. She had three grandchildren back east. Her husband had died five years ago. She now spent her time writing and gardening. Elmer brought her up to date about his last fifty years, embellishing his accomplishments a little.

Before long the conversation turned to their high school days. They talked about their favorite teachers, what had happened to friends that weren't at the reunion, and recounted fragments of scandals from fifty years ago. Elmer began to relax and enjoy the conversation.

They had played in the school band together, and laughed over an incident when Susan had accused Elmer of swapping her music with that of the tuba player. He hadn't done it, but even having her mad at him had been a thrill at the time. Elmer reminded Susan of the brief conversations they usually had while they were waiting in the hall for the director to open the music room before band practice. Elmer didn't tell Susan that those precious few minutes every day had been the main focus of much of his high school career.

Susan remarked in passing that she always wondered, back then, why Elmer never asked her for a date, speculating that he must have had a girlfriend he never mentioned. She thought the comment was unremarkable; Elmer was speechless. He let her continue making small talk for a minute while he collected his wits. He had a girlfriend he never mentioned all right!

"Susan, are you telling me you would have gone out with me if I had asked?" Elmer inquired cautiously.

"Of course, why wouldn't I? You were SO smart and funny! I had a little crush on you back then; didn't you know?"

Elmer wasn't sure whether to laugh or cry so he just sat there for a minute looking at her, his mouth agape.

"Elmer, what are you thinking?" she asked softly, guessing correctly by the look on Elmer's face the general outline of his thoughts.

Elmer gave her a look that slightly resembled a smile. "I'm thinking I could use another gin and tonic. Would you like something?"

"I think a gin and tonic would be a very good idea right now, thank you."

Elmer brought the drinks and the conversation continued on a somewhat more intimate level, but neither wanted to delve too deeply into the implications of Elmer's adolescent reticence. Elmer had found himself wiping his eye with his handkerchief while he was waiting for the drinks, but by the time he got back to the table he felt wonderful. They had a witty and lively conversation about life, grandchildren, interpersonal relationships, and his dad's old Ford, although Elmer didn't mention everything he was thinking about that subject.

Across the room, Tilly had found Buff holding court with several of their former classmates. She had looked him up on the internet a few months earlier and knew that he had become a minister, a fact that seemed strange when applied to the Buff Stevens she remembered. In any case, he had built up a large following and had become quite wealthy from the sale of his book, *Achieving God's Full Blessings Through Strict Marital Fidelity*. When she arrived at his circle of admirers she was taken aback. Buff now appeared to weigh about four hundred pounds and used a walker to help support himself even when he was standing still. He was apparently a cigar smoker because he had several in his pocket and a disagreeable smoky aroma surrounding him. He was wearing an expensive suit and a cheap toupee.

"Milly!" he bellowed when she arrived, and he skidded forward to give her a bear hug, banging her knee with his walker.

"It's Tilly!" she said.

"No, it's Milly!" he reiterated. "Unless I'm mixing you up with someone else. Did you and I sneak over the fence at the swimming pool in the park one night and go skinny-dipping at one in the morning?"

"That must have been 'Milly'!" frowned Tilly.

"Maybe so. Anyway, what have you been up to these last fifty years?" asked Buff.

"Well, I married Elmer Talbot after college and —"

"I got married too, six times!" laughed Buff. "Got tired of the same old thing every night, you know how it is! Do you and Elmo have any kids?"

"Three," replied Tilly.

"I have ten that I know of," said Buff. "There could be a few more somewhere, but only ten that hang around me looking for a handout. Have you and Elmo read my book?"

"No," replied Tilly.

"You should! It could save your marriage! You can get it on Amazon for $29.95."

Tilly thought that Buff had already begun to improve her marriage since Elmer was looking better and better to her each time Buff opened his mouth.

Tilly was treated to a detailed description of Buff's house, in Omaha, "Just down the block from Warren Buffett", and his other house in Florida. He let her in on private information about his net worth and how stupid he thought most of his readers were. He described many of the works in his collection of paintings of Jesus on velvet. He complained about the trips to Italy he had to make several times a year to buy suits because tailors in New York couldn't seem to make suits to fit him.

"At least the trips are deductible!" he laughed.

He gave an intimate account of his love life, including the fact that he could only date thin women because he had to have the interior of his Porsche customized to widen the driver's seat, which only left room for a small passenger.

Finally, someone announced that dinner was being served and asked everyone to find the seat with their name card on it. As Tilly was taking her leave, Buff put his arm around her, conspiratorially.

"I have a couple of bottles of Chivas Regal in my hotel room. Why don't the two of us head over there for a nightcap, or a night, after this shindig?"

"No thanks," said Tilly. "I don't think Elmo would approve!"

At dinner, it was Tilly's turn to be grumpy. Luckily, both Buff and Susan were seated at other tables.

When Elmer asked Tilly about Buff she just said, "I'll tell you later."

After an unexceptional meal, and an hour of sitting through speeches by former classmates who overvalued their public speaking talents, it was time to go home. As they were leaving, Susan and Elmer gave each other a parting hug, the duration of which was much longer than Tilly thought absolutely necessary. Tilly pointed out Buff, arm in arm with one of his admirers, to Elmer.

On the way home, Tilly snuggled up next to her husband.

"Susan is STILL very cute isn't she?" asked Tilly, hoping for a denial.

"Yes," laughed Elmer. "She and I had a very intimate relationship for a few years. You're lucky she didn't know anything about it!"

"I'm sorry I teased you about Buff," Tilly said. "He turned out to be a real jerk. In fact, you were the handsomest man in the room tonight. I can't wait to get naked in bed with you!"

"That's funny," chuckled Elmer. "Susan said the same thing!"

"SHE WHAT?"

"Just teasing!" said Elmer as he gently placed his hand on Tilly's thigh.

As it had when she was eighteen, Elmer's hand on her leg caused a wave of sexual arousal to wash over Tilly. Elmer felt it at the same time.

"Elmer?"

"Yes."

"I don't think I can wait until we get home to make love to you," said Tilly.

"Well, there's always the lane behind Old Man Smith's hedgerow," suggested Elmer.

Tilly smiled. "Great idea! That's a perfect location for our personal fiftieth reunion. Do you still remember all those romantic moves you made on me when we used to park there back in high school?"

"Of course!" grinned Elmer. "In fact, I've been going over them in my mind all evening!"

~~~
~~~

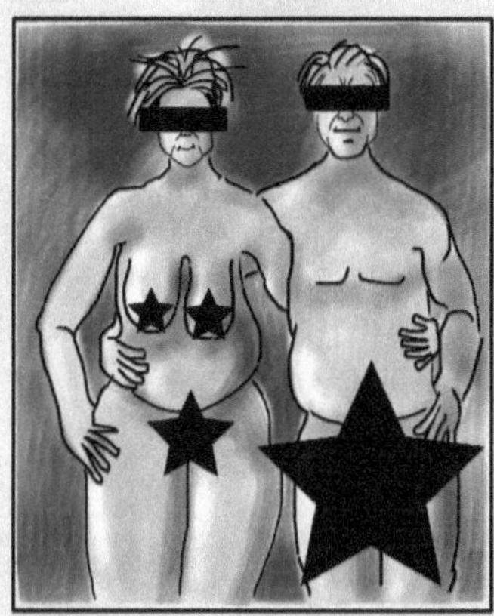

South Branch Sentinel
"All the News We Think Will Sell Newspapers"

Local Couple Caught in Las Vegas Sex Scandal

Local couple, Tilly and Elmer Talbot, were caught by a photographer having sex in the window of a Las Vegas hotel room last weekend. Their photograph has gone viral on the internet and the city council is considering whether to erect a statue in the park honoring Elmer as the greatest stud west of the Mississippi.

TILLY AND ELMER GO TO LAS VEGAS

"I fucked that fuckin' bitch three fuckin' times, dude!"

Pearl looked up and frowned in the direction of a boisterous group of high school boys as she wiped the front counter. The discussion of carburetors between Elmer and his friends at the "geezers' table" fell silent.

"Three fuckin' times? NO FUCKIN' WAY!"

"Shit, I could have fucked her a couple more times, but she had to fuckin' go home early."

"Where the fuck WAS this, dude?"

"In the fuckin' dugout at the field. Hey slugger,

you'd better watch out for the sticky spot when you're warmin' the fuckin' bench this afternoon."

"Damn, dude, I thought she was too high-and-mighty for any of us. You must be the greatest fuckin' stud west of the Mississippi! They should put up a fuckin' statue of you in the fuckin' park or something!"

Pearl peered over the tops of her reading glasses and gave the boys an authoritative look. They bustled out, pushing each other and laughing. Gradually, the conversation picked up again at the "geezers' table." Now the topic was a rehash of stories they had told each other many times before about their own teenage love affairs. As usual, the stories were a combination of a little reality and a lot of fantasy that they had forgotten hadn't actually happened.

By the time Elmer got home, he was depressed.

"How's everything in town?" asked Tilly.

"OK, I guess."

"What's the matter?"

Elmer was usually happy to recount the latest gossip and idle chat from Pearl's Main Street Diner.

"A bunch of high school kids were in Pearl's this morning, talking about their girlfriends. It made me feel a hundred years old."

"I wouldn't worry," said Tilly. "You're pretty hot for a centenarian."

"I don't feel that hot," replied Elmer.

"Well, I just saw an ad on TV for something that will cure that," Tilly told him.

"Does it involve us putting two claw foot bathtubs next to each other out in the back yard?" asked Elmer.

"No, it involves plane tickets to Las Vegas," laughed Tilly.

"I don't know, Tilly. We did have fun the last time we were in Las Vegas, but that was thirty years ago. Those twenty-something showgirls with tits out to here weren't that much younger than I was back then.

Now I think they would just depress me more."

"Maybe we can find you some eighty-year-old showgirls, Elmer. That should turn on a centenarian like you," chuckled Tilly. Elmer managed a smile.

"Eighty-year-old show girls don't excite me like they did twenty years ago," he complained.

He began to warm up to the Las Vegas idea when he remembered how, the last time they were there, Tilly had talked him into pretending she was a complete stranger one evening. She made him arrive in the bar separately, then try to pick her up and take her to his room. Of course he was successful, after what he thought was an unnecessary amount of sweet talk, but he wasn't sure whether to be annoyed or proud when Tilly later told him another guy had tried to pick her up before he got there. Elmer told himself she had probably made that story up anyway.

"Ok, I suppose it could be fun. But you may have to help me fight off the eighty-year-old, sex crazed women," said Elmer.

"Just run over their toes with your walker – that will discourage them," advised Tilly.

Las Vegas was quite a bit different than it had been when they were last there. They had been in their late thirties at the time, and loved the bright lights and fast pace. This time, they moved slower and Las Vegas moved faster. On the other hand, Tilly was delighted to find that there were lots of wonderful restaurants in place of the mediocre buffets they remembered. Elmer was more concerned with the sky-high prices than the gourmet food, but he figured that they could manage it once every thirty years. They made a reservation at a fancy restaurant and went off to explore the strip. The first thing they noticed was the cast of characters and their attire. Half the population seemed to be dressed for a fancy party; the other half seemed dressed to get arrested for indecent exposure. Elmer had never paid much attention to fashion, but he did notice some of the fashions, or lack of fashions, on their fellow strollers.

He was especially taken by a woman his age, seriously overweight, wearing spiked heels, a purple bra, and bike shorts, surmounted by a tutu, garter belt, and stockings to match her bra. He wondered if she had just forgotten to finish getting dressed; he had done that himself on occasion, but somehow he didn't think so.

As he was marveling at the variety of fashions, Tilly took his arm, changing their direction and leading him into a nearby dress shop.

"I'm not going into that fancy restaurant in this old dress," she announced.

Before Elmer could protest, his eye was caught by a sparkly red dress in the window.

"Tilly would look nice in that!" he thought.

The red dress didn't appeal to Tilly, but after trying on several party dresses, a process that Elmer complained about, but secretly enjoyed, she chose a black silky top and matching skirt that flowed around her legs like bourbon appears to flow around your glass in slow motion when you've had one too many. She looked beautiful.

"I must say, Tilly, you'll give those eighty-year-olds some pretty stiff competition in that dress."

"And I'm counting on you to give me something stiff once I get out of it," purred Tilly.

"Besides a drink, you mean?" chuckled Elmer.

"In addition to a drink!" whispered Tilly into his good ear.

Elmer spent extra time getting dressed for the evening's dinner. It took him nearly ten minutes to get his look just right. Not so with Tilly. When she finally emerged from the bathroom, Elmer was stunned. Not only did the dress look even better than it had when she tried it on, she had put on just a bit of makeup and done something a little different with her hair, although Elmer couldn't quite tell what it was.

"Wow, you look great!" he told her.

"You ain't seen nothin' yet," chuckled Tilly.

Elmer couldn't figure out what she meant, but he liked what he had seen so far.

"Those eighty-year-olds might as well stay home, I'm bringing YOU home with me tonight, stranger."

"You sure are, big boy!" smiled Tilly.

They got to the restaurant a little early and decided to wait in the bar until their table was ready, choosing a hideaway in the darkest corner.

As Elmer was pulling out Tilly's chair, she leaned over and said in a low voice, "Just in the interest of full disclosure, I'm not wearing any panties."

Elmer's jaw dropped. He'd always imagined her going out in public sans underwear, but she'd never done it before as far as he could remember, and he was pretty sure he would have remembered such an occasion. Elmer was a little distracted when the waitress came to take their order. He decided to celebrate the news with an expensive scotch. Tilly had some kind of drink that was bright blue. There was a little light in the base of her glass that made the concoction look like neon. As they were enjoying the drinks, Tilly reached under the table and slid her skirt up to mid thigh. Forgetting where they were, Elmer picked up Tilly's drink and positioned it like a lantern in the hand of an ancient mariner so he could see better.

He was enjoying the sight of her thighs glowing bright blue, but he set the glass back on the table quickly, once he realized he was on the verge of letting everyone in the bar in on her secret. Tilly took Elmer's hand and placed it under her skirt, just below the tops of her thigh highs. She guided his hand up her thigh as she leaned over and whispered that she had another

secret waiting for him.

Elmer was completely baffled. The secret she had already revealed, and that he was about to verify, seemed to cover all the possibilities.

Whatever the next secret was, Elmer was ready with a mixture of anticipation, nervousness, and confusion. Soft music played in the background as Tilly took her sweet time easing his hand up her inner thigh. Tilly was smiling from ear to ear as she enjoyed teasing Elmer, who was speechless by this time. Finally, she softly pressed the side of his hand between her legs. Elmer's eyes opened wide.

"TILLY!" he said a little too loudly.

"Yes, Elmer?" she murmured softly.

Looking around quickly to be sure no one was listening, he stammered, "You shaved down there?"

"You noticed, did you?" Tilly teased.

"Where did you get that idea?" said Elmer in disbelief.

"I don't subscribe to *Woman's Night* magazine for nothing. Shaving that area is all the fashion nowadays."

"But.... Tilly, I never imagined..."

"Come on Elmer!" laughed Tilly. "I know you've seen pictures of all kinds of women on the internet with shaved pubic areas."

"Sure, but ... I never imagined...you."

"You can do more than imagine after dinner, Elmer, but for now, our table's ready!"

Although Elmer hardly tasted the food, it was the best dinner he remembered having in ages. The plates consisted of a few artistically arranged morsels, which suited Elmer fine since he couldn't wait for the dinner to be over. Tilly, however, savored each bite in the most sensual way, giving the impression she was about to have an orgasm with each mouthful. She insisted on sharing a chocolate creation for dessert, and for a while Elmer thought she was getting so aroused by the concoction that he would be an afterthought when the meal was done. She assured him otherwise by slipping a spoonful of the dessert into his mouth and telling him that it was the second most delicious thing he was going to taste that night.

They walked, holding hands, back to the hotel room, stopping for a kiss every now and then. Elmer couldn't remember a nicer evening. When they reached the room, Elmer turned on the lamp on the table by the window. Tilly started to close the curtains, but Elmer stopped her.

"It's such a nice night, let's leave the curtains open."

"But Elmer, there are three hundred hotel rooms across the street looking right into our window!"

"Well, all those people have their own affairs to worry about. They won't be interested in a one hundred-year-old man getting it on with an eighty-year-old show girl."

"I don't know, Elmer!" Tilly said as they looked out the window.

He stood behind her and unbuttoned her top.

"They could all be looking at us," she said.

Elmer removed Tilly's top and slipped off her bra.

"They're too far away to see anything," he said.

"Do you think so?" asked Tilly, unconvinced.

She bent over and put her hands on the window sill, attempting to see anyone who might be watching them. Elmer unbuckled his pants and let them fall to the floor, then lifted her skirt.

"Well, they won't see anything unless they have binoculars," he teased.

"OH, ELMER! I'll bet some of them DO have binoculars!"

He began to make love to her from behind, easing into a familiar rhythm.

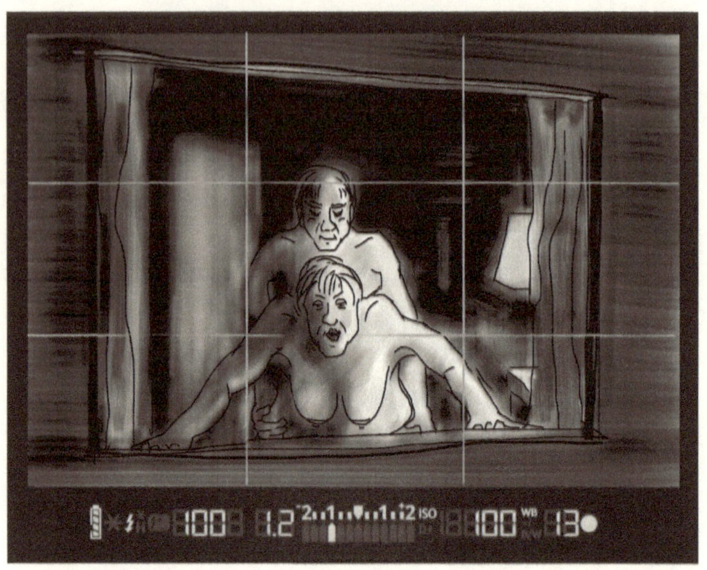

"And the rest have cameras," mentioned Elmer, a little out of breath.

"Oh My God, Elmer!" Tilly moaned. "What if they're taking pictures of you fucking me right here in the window?"

Tilly didn't use that word often, but Elmer knew it was a good sign when she did.

"What ... um ... what would ... uh (pant) what would they want, *Oh God Elmer*, (pant) *Ohhhh fuck!* ... want with, *ahhhh*, (pant) fucking, *ummmm*, (sharp intake of breath) ... pictures?"

"They'd want to put them on the internet of course," said Elmer, nearly out of breath.

"OHHH MYYY GODDDD, ELMER!!!" wailed Tilly, quivering with a mixture of concern, shock, and pleasure.

When the morning sun woke them up, Tilly and Elmer found themselves on the floor by the window. The bed was untouched.

"I guess we wore each other out last night," smiled Elmer.

"I guess we did. You have a lot of stamina for a centenarian," teased Tilly.

She rolled over and gave him a long, romantic kiss.

"I can't believe we did it with the curtains open," she said. "Do you really think people across the way could have been taking pictures of us?"

"I hope so," said Elmer.

"YOU HOPE SO? Elmer, what if they put pictures of us on the internet and they end up on the front page of the *South Branch Sentinel* or something?"

"That would be great!"

"ELMER! How can you say that? It would be very embarrassing!"

"No it wouldn't!" replied Elmer "If our picture was on the front page of the *South Branch Sentinel*, my buddies down at Pearl's would have to agree I was the greatest stud west of the Mississippi, instead of that 'smart aleck' high school kid that was down there last week. They might even erect a statue of me in the park to commemorate that achievement."

Tilly began to laugh, literally rolling on the floor.

"Well, big boy, if they ever make a statue of you based on a picture from last night, there will be plenty of space for the pigeons to roost."

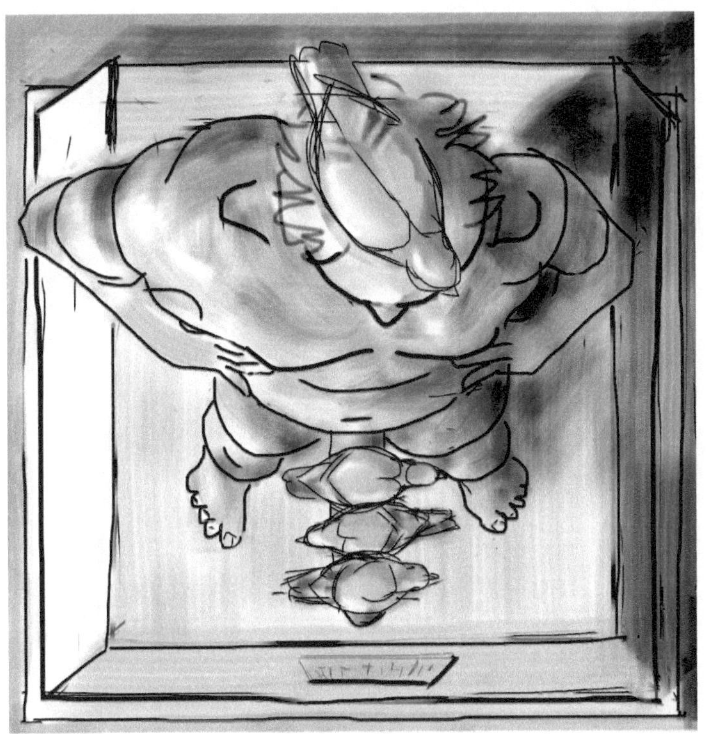

~~~
~~~

TILLY AND ELMER GET CRAZY

"I got you new batteries for your hearing aid," Tilly said, as they started home from town in Elmer's old pickup.

"What?" replied Elmer.

Tilly just smiled as she took her new magazine, *Woman's Excitement,* out of the grocery bag. As usual, the cover promised romantic advice. This month it was, "Four Ways to Drive your Man Crazy in the Bedroom." Tilly wondered if it also included instructions on keeping him from being crazy the rest of the time.

"Listen to this, Elmer," she said, "Here's an article on how I can drive you crazy in bed!"

"You already drive me crazy in bed Tilly!" said Elmer with a grin. "Like when you mention that the bedroom ceiling needs painting just when I'm about to finish making love to you."

"Not crazy that way, silly," said Tilly. "I mean how to make you wildly sexually excited!"

"What does it recommend?" asked Elmer.

"Tip Number 1, Do What he Loved When You Were First Dating!"

"I'll SHOW you!" laughed Tilly as they reached the railroad tracks at the edge of town. She raised herself up off the seat, pulled her skirt up, and slipped off her panties. Elmer was beginning to like this article.

"I thought you said, 'Drive your man crazy in bed,' not 'bed your man while he's driving.'"

"You didn't see anything dangerous about it when we were eighteen," Tilly laughed.

"Well, in my defense, I was driving as slowly as I could back then because I wanted to keep you out as late as possible."

Tilly slid over next to Elmer and put her hand on his thigh. The restored truck, the same one Elmer had when they were dating, had a manual transmission with the shift lever on the floor. Tilly straddled the shift knob, just like she used to do, so that Elmer's hand was between her legs whenever he had to shift

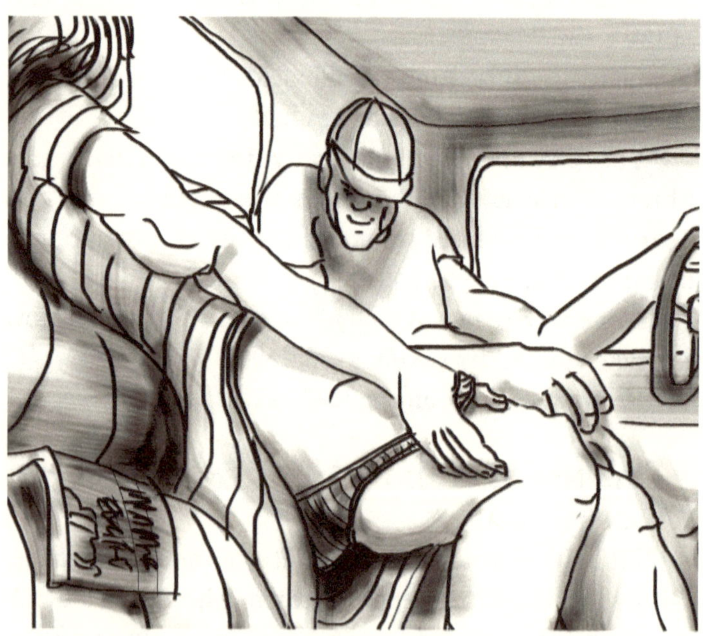

into first or third. It seemed to her that he had to shift more often when they were dating, but the lever still vibrated just like it always did which made each gear change even more fun for her.

"What do you say to taking the long way home and pulling over behind Old Man Smith's hedgerow like we used to?" said Elmer.

"No, it wouldn't be proper," said Tilly. "And besides, I have to get the milk, eggs, and bacon into the fridge before they spoil."

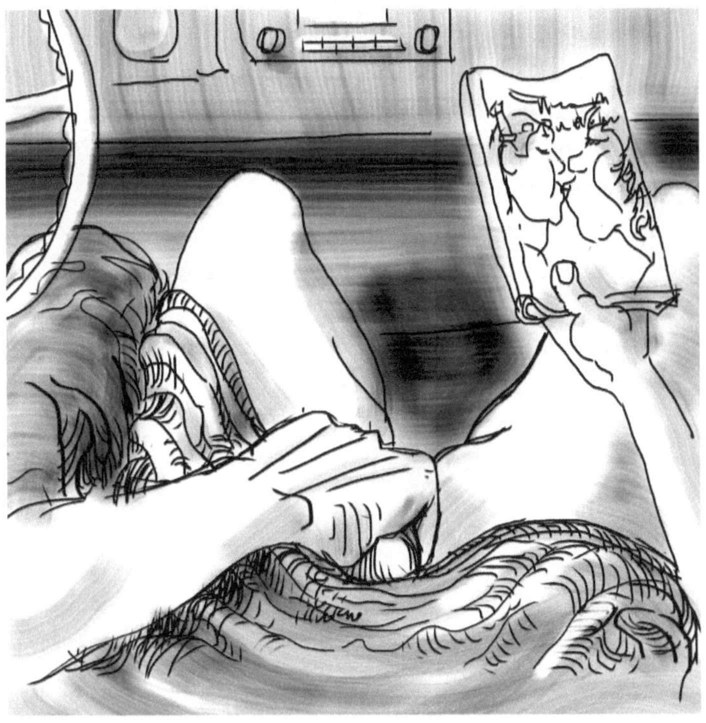

"It wasn't 'proper' then either," replied Elmer, "but I didn't notice that stopping us. Still, I have to do a couple of chores when I get home so I guess we'll have to wait."

Tilly went back to her reading, now and then reacting with a small giggle or gasp to the suggestions. They had planned to have lunch before they left town, but they had both forgotten about that idea.

"Don't be too long with those chores, honey!" teased Tilly as they pulled into the lane.

Elmer went to feed the pigs, laughing at the rear view of a half dozen of them, jostling for the best spot at the food trough, curly tails wagging like puppies. When he finished, he got undressed as usual on the back porch, hung his overalls on the hook, and took a quick rinse in the outdoor shower. Now to see what Tilly had in mind.

Elmer found Tilly waiting for him in the bedroom, but he wasn't fully prepared for her second idea.

"Tip Number 2, Try a new look!"

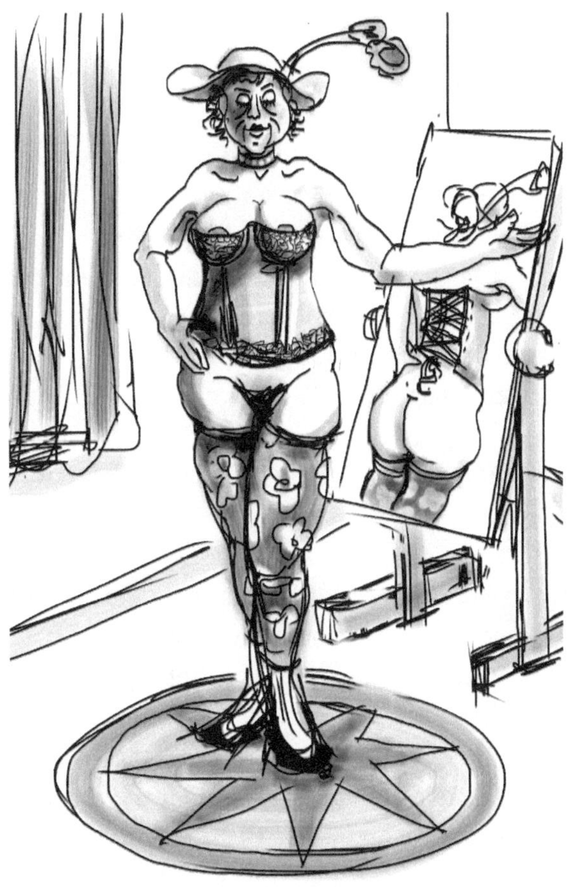

Tilly modeled her creative fashion statement. The centerpiece of the outfit was a lacy corset she had found in an old trunk in the closet. Faded pink in color, it laced up the back. It was a bit wider in fit now than it was when she last wore it forty years ago, but it had driven him crazy then, and was a good start this time. On her head, Tilly wore a straw hat with a peacock feather that she had gotten from her grandmother. Around her neck was a leather collar that normally belonged to their dog, Alex. For her midsection, she had chosen – nothing. She wore dark flowered tights with the top portion cut off to make leggings reaching to the tops of her thighs. On her feet were bobby socks and patent leather flats.

Elmer was speechless; she had all his favorites on at the same time. He revealed that her plan had worked and suggested they climb into bed.

"Not yet!" said Tilly. "You aren't crazy enough."

"Tip Number 3, Let go of Your Inhibitions and Dance for Him!"

Tilly wasn't known for her dancing, but she seemed to have gotten into the spirit of the article. She required Elmer to disrobe and settle back into the rocking chair they kept in the bedroom before beginning her performance. The dance included a number of moves involving undulating breasts quite near Elmer's face and hula like shimmying of Tilly's bottom. She incorporated quite a few slow, loving, touches of Elmer's body, which did seem to have the effect of diminishing his sanity. He doubted Tilly could find work in the erotic dance field, but her performance was having the desired effect on him, that was for sure.

"That article was pretty accurate," whispered Elmer. "I believe you'll find me sufficiently crazy at this point."

"I'm just getting started, lover boy!" smiled Tilly.

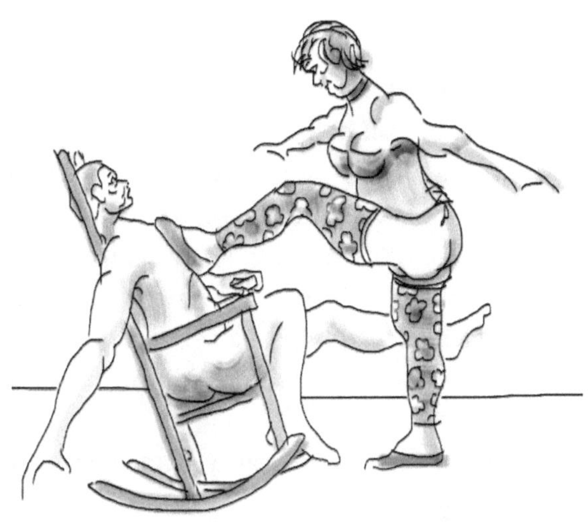

"Tip Number 4, Slip Something Sweet Into his Mouth!"

Tilly pushed Elmer down on the bed and sat astride his midsection, facing him. She had prepared a bowl of fruit and slowly inserted a peach slice into his mouth. Apparently peaches worked as well as Viagra! After a few of these, Tilly picked out a short piece of peeled banana, took one end into her mouth and leaned over, slipping the other end into Elmer's mouth. They nibbled their way to a kiss. Getting into the game, Elmer found another peach slice and touched it to the exposed part of Tilly's breasts, then pulled her closer so he could lick the juice off. Elmer began to feel he had been driven just about crazy enough for one afternoon and was definitely ready to move on to whatever the next step was.

"DAMMIT!" said Tilly.

"What's the matter?"

"I forgot the melon balls."

"Forget the MELON balls!" advised Elmer. "I have two balls right here that are about to burst!"

"No, I have to follow the instructions if I'm going to drive you crazy!" Tilly got up and went into the kitchen. Elmer followed. Alex gave out a howl.

"Is she driving you crazy too?" Elmer asked him.

Tilly opened the refrigerator and bent over to retrieve the forgotten melon.

"She still has the world's cutest ass," Elmer thought.

The little tie at the bottom of her corset looked like a curly tail, and with her soft round rump, reminded him of his earlier chores. Out of the blue he remembered that the word "bacon" comes from the German word for "buttocks." Elmer laughed out loud.

"What's so funny?" asked Tilly.

Elmer knew better than to reveal the reason he was laughing. "I was wondering if we have ever had sex in the refrigerator," he said.

"Keep your pants on, big boy – I mean figuratively since you aren't wearing any. I'm going to drive you crazy no matter how crazy that drives you."

"Those melon balls had better be pretty good,"

thought Elmer. Then he thought, "I wonder what she intends to do with them."

As Elmer contemplated various ways they could use melon balls as sex toys, his gaze slid up the tight lacing of Tilly's corset, along her back, and across her bare shoulders. Her grey hair glowed in the light of the refrigerator bulb, which also illuminated a package next to the Dr. Pepper.

"Is that bacon?" Elmer wondered.

He suddenly remembered they had missed lunch.

As Tilly was making balls out of the melon at the sink, she heard a sizzling sound. Elmer was frying a half dozen bacon slices.

"OH MY GOD! What are you doing?" shouted Tilly.

"Frying Bacon," said Elmer, matter-of-factly.

"I can see you're frying bacon. I mean what are you doing frying bacon NAKED! Put on my apron before you sizzle your own bacon! It's in the drawer next to you."

"Good idea!" said Elmer.

"I'll say!" said Tilly. "I wouldn't want you to damage anything with hot grease!"

Elmer put on the little white apron. He looked ridiculous. The white fabric draped over his erection like a dishcloth hung over the kitchen faucet. Tilly set the bowl of melon balls in the sink. The little twitching white apron sticking out in front of Elmer had the same effect on her as a red cape waving in front of a bull.

You look very cute in that apron, Elmer. I don't know if we've ever done it in the refrigerator, but I know we're about to do it on the kitchen floor!"

Elmer turned off the bacon, and Tilly took his hand and lowered him to the little rug in front of the stove. She squealed and climbed on top of him.

"Seeing you in that sexy little apron is a huge turn on."

"That's interesting!" Elmer thought to himself, seeing the wild look in Tilly's eyes. "I may have to write a magazine article on how to drive your woman crazy in the kitchen!"

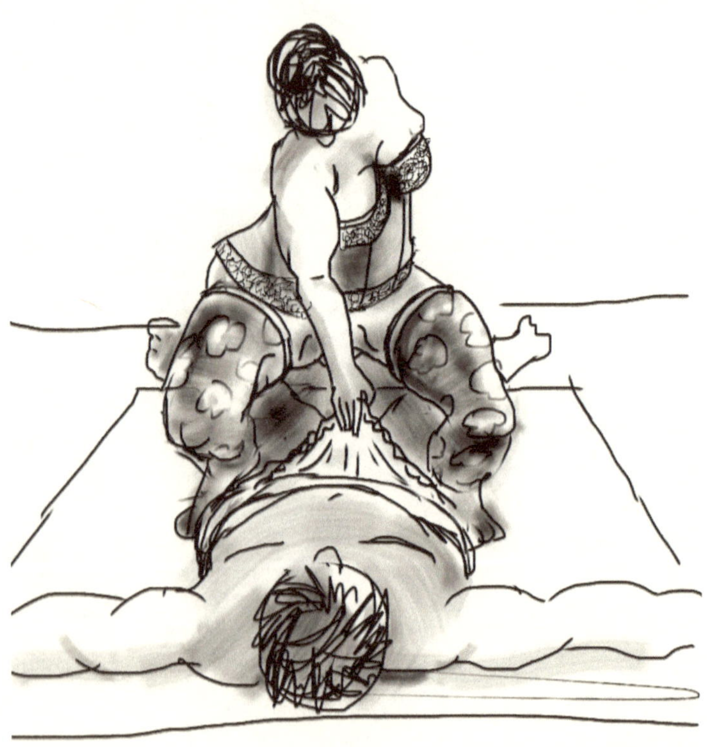

~ ~ ~

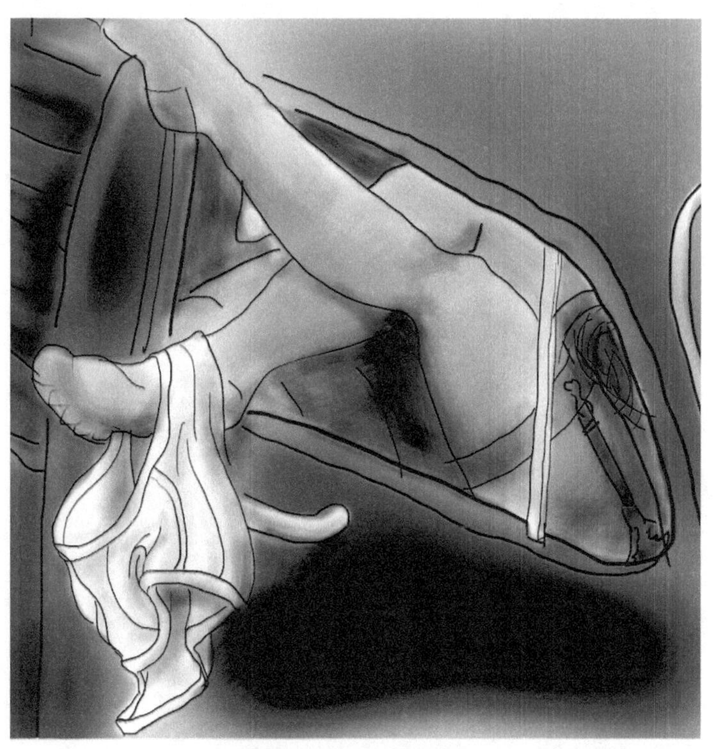

TRUCK TRYST

"Elmer, I'm home," announced Tilly.

Elmer looked up from the paper. "How was the card game?"

"I had lousy cards, but you'll never guess what I heard! Sally told us how she and Al turned up the heat on their sex life."

"Is that what you girls talk about while you're supposed to be playing bridge?"

"Of course, you don't think we're trading recipes all afternoon, do you?" laughed Tilly. Elmer had a disconcerting moment wondering if Tilly's girlfriends were, at that moment, telling their husbands about Elmer's little issue last Thursday evening.

"Sally told us she and Al did it on the front porch last Saturday night! Even though you can't see their house that well from the road, she said it was really exciting."

"Did you tell them all about our sex life?" Elmer asked cautiously.

"Not in too much detail!" grinned Tilly. Elmer wondered how much detail was too much.

"On TV they say you should get out of your marital routine sometimes to, you know, perk up your privates."

"I think my privates are perky enough. Most of the time, anyway," muttered Elmer. "I like our regular routine just fine. Besides, we don't have a front porch."

'I know," said Tilly, "but we have your old truck. Remember the fun we used to have in that truck down by Old Man Smith's orchard?"

"You're right about that, Tilly," said Elmer. "But as

I recall, we wished we could just climb into a big bed together every time we had to squeeze into that little cab."

"Come on, Elmer. We can do it in bed any time. Let's give that old truck a workout tonight like we used to."

Elmer could see that Tilly was determined to carry out her plan, and he did have fond memories of that old truck.

"OK, Tilly, I'll do it with you in the truck on two conditions," said Elmer.

"OK, I won't lean back against the horn again like that one time," promised Tilly. "I think it took you a week to get another erection after that."

"I guess that makes three conditions," laughed Elmer. "Can we just drive the truck up behind the house? I don't want to be out in somebody's pasture when we do it."

"Ok, if you're chicken, I guess I can live with that. What's the other condition?"

"You have to dress up like you did when we used to do it in the truck. Tight sweater, skirt with those puffy slip things..."

"Crinolines."

"Right, crinolines. And white cotton panties, garter belt, stockings. The full regalia."

"You hated that stuff at the time; it took too long to get it off!" Tilly reminded him.

"Well, I love it now, 'Flash!' And I have all the time in the world to get it off, to coin a phrase. Is it a deal?"

"You drive a hard bargain, 'Wiggle Bear', but since

you called me 'Flash' just like you used to when we were in school, I'll go for it!"

She hadn't called him "Wiggle Bear" since high school. Elmer could feel his privates perking up already.

After dinner, Tilly did the best she could to reproduce her old schoolgirl outfit. It wasn't perfect but it had the main elements, even though some of the older pieces were significantly tighter than they would have been back then. She hoped Elmer could get them off in the confined space of the truck cab. For his part, Elmer found an old white T-shirt from when he was thinner and a pair of old jeans that were a tight fit. Perfect.

Elmer parked the truck behind the house, out of sight of the road or any of the neighbors. He knocked on the kitchen door and Tilly came out, pretending to call goodbye to her parents as she would have when they were dating. Elmer helped her into the truck, then climbed in behind the wheel. There was a moment of awkwardness, just like in the old days. Then it was because they were still learning what to do. Now they just didn't know what to do first.

Tilly slid over next to Elmer and turned toward him. Elmer turned to face her, his tight pants giving him an unpleasant squeeze.

"Ow!"

"What's the matter?"

"I just have to rearrange things a bit."

"Let me help. Those pants have to come off before

something gets damaged," purred Tilly.

Elmer leaned over to untie his shoes, but the steering wheel was in his way. With some discomfort, he leaned back against the driver's door and stretched his legs out on the floor toward Tilly. She leaned over to untie them, but couldn't quite bend down that way. She did manage to lift his legs one at a time onto the seat so she could take off his shoes. She managed to get on her knees on the seat facing him and began on his pants.

The tight jeans were a struggle, but with Elmer pushing down one side and then the other a half inch at a time, and Tilly pulling from the cuffs, they eventually came off, taking his boxers along with them. They were both breathing heavily, but not for the same reason they used to when Elmer's pants came off.

Elmer grabbed the seat back and the steering wheel and lifted himself to a more upright position. He attempted to bend his right knee and slip his leg between Tilly's thigh and the seat back, but there was no space there so he bent his knee further and located his foot in front of her knee. Now for that sweater. His leg position, however, wouldn't allow him to lean far enough forward to lift the bottom of Tilly's sweater so she slipped it over her head and tossed it over the steering wheel. Tilly put her hand on Elmer's knee and began to lift her hips so she could lean over and kiss Elmer's chest. Her head hit the ceiling of the truck. She tried bending over without raising up that far, and was able to lean over Elmer so he could reach around and unfasten her bra. He remembered when he could do that with one hand, just with a clever movement of his thumb and forefinger. This time, it took both hands and a bit of fumbling. As he was finally removing her bra, Tilly's right leg began to cramp; she leaned against Elmer's raised knee and gently moved her leg down off the seat so she could straighten it out.

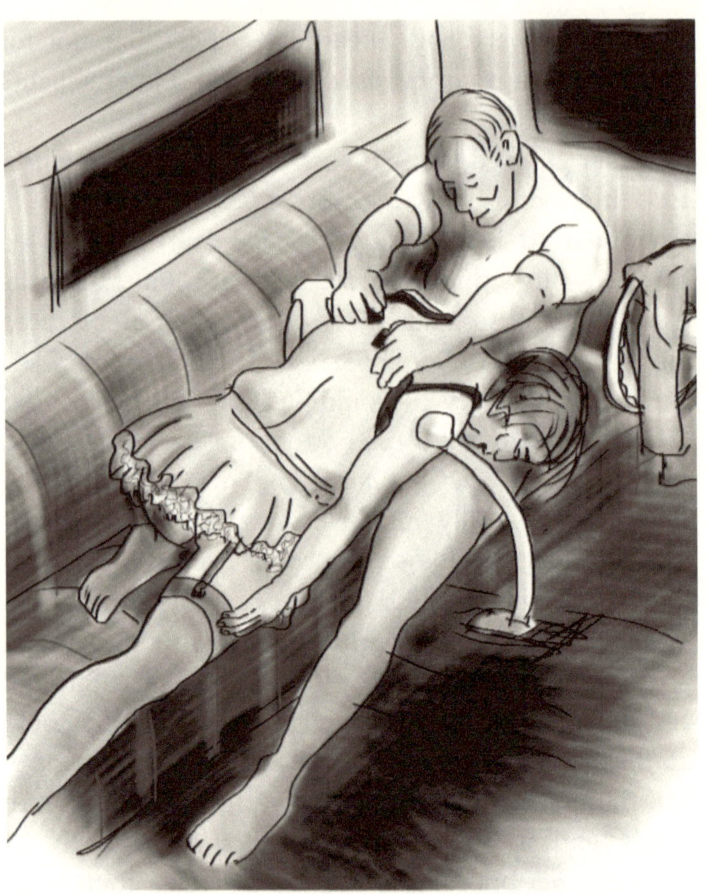

Tilly couldn't remember any problems at all when she and Elmer were in Old Man Smith's lane. After the cramp in her leg subsided, Tilly moved her right knee to the edge of the passenger seat and slowly turned to face the seat back so Elmer could lie down on his side, facing her. Elmer pulled himself up onto his knee. As he twisted to lay down on his side along the seat, he felt a sharp pain in his back.

"OWWWW! Dammit!"

"What happened?" Tilly asked.

"I twisted something in my back. I don't think I can move."

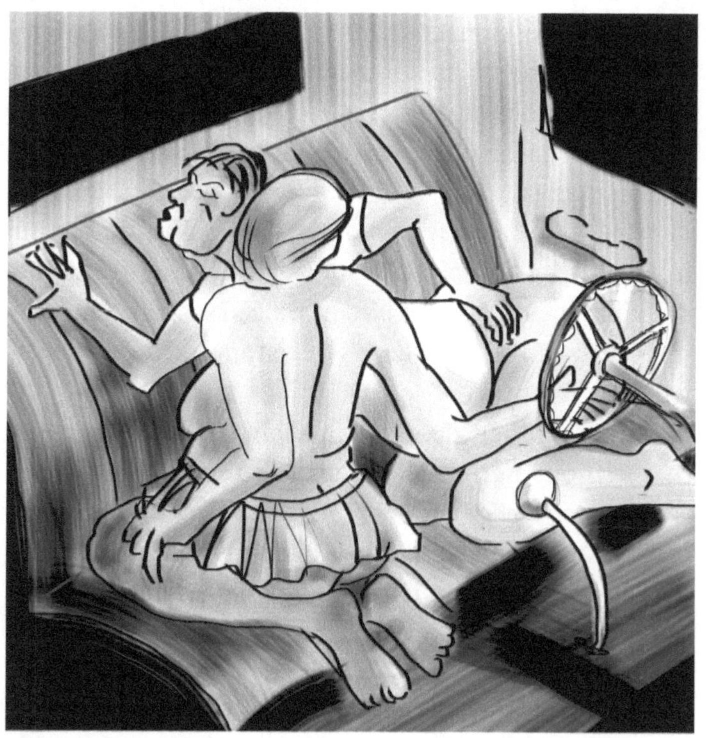

Tilly had been a nurse before she retired, so she knew what to do. She helped him into the house, suppressing a chuckle at the picture they made. It was a good thing they weren't parked where anyone could see the truck since she was naked above the waist and Elmer was naked from the waist down. She got Elmer into bed and took off his shirt. He felt a little better after the glass of medicine she brought him, especially since it was brandy.

"I'm feeling a little better. I think I could get up now," said Elmer cautiously.

"Not yet!" said Tilly, "Remember, I'm a trained medical professional."

She left the room for a few minutes, and returned wearing her old nurse's cap. Tilly lifted the front of her skirt to reveal that she was still wearing the garter belt and stockings.

"I'm glad to see it was only your back and not your front that was affected!" smiled Tilly. She went into the kitchen and poured two more glasses of brandy.

"Can you roll over onto your stomach?" Tilly asked when she returned.

After another dose of medicine, Elmer managed that without a grimace. "See, all better!" he said.

"Not so fast, big boy!" said Tilly in her most professional tone. "I have to finish my examination."

Tilly opened the drawer of her nightstand and took out her vibrator.

"What's that for?" asked Elmer.

"You feel hot so I'd better take your temperature. It's a rectal thermometer," said Tilly matter-of-factly.

"Tilly, that's your dildo!" Elmer pointed out, nervously.

"No, it's a rectal thermometer," Tilly asserted. "I already told you I was a trained professional. Sorry, doctor's orders."

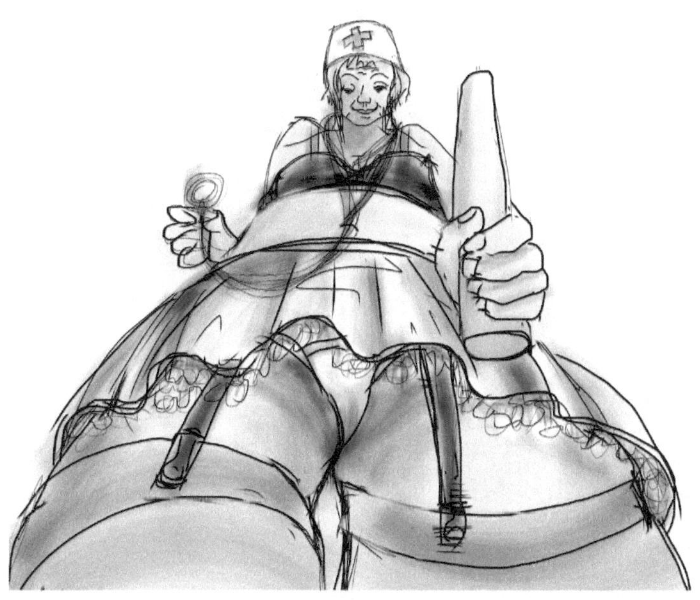

"But…"

"Yes, Elmer, that IS where you use a rectal thermometer."

Fortunately, Elmer didn't have a fever after all. Tilly gently rubbed his back.

"You know Elmer, a fever can come on any time. I think I'd better give you a routine check-up like this from time to time."

"I think you'd better," said Elmer. "I told you there was nothing wrong with a regular routine."

~~~
~~~

TILLY AND ELMER GET WARMED UP

Elmer came in from the barn, brushing the snow off his jacket.

"Tilly, it's a beautiful day outside!"

"A beautiful day for staying inside you mean? Isn't it freezing out there?"

"No, the sun is out and the snow is still powdery and soft. It's beautiful."

Tilly looked out the kitchen window. Last night's

snow was smooth and glistening in the winter sun. The landscape looked like it was covered by a huge white down comforter. Elmer was grinning in a way she had seen before.

"OK, Elmer, you have something in mind don't you? You've got that look in your eye and you're touching my butt. Shall we slip into the bedroom for a little while?"

"Tilly, remember fifty years ago, before we were married and —"

"I think we both remember fifty years and fifty pounds ago, yes," laughed Tilly.

"— and that time we went out into the woods when it was snowy like this?" continued Elmer.

Tilly raised her left eyebrow. "You're not suggesting we —?"

"Sure I am. We haven't played around in the woods for years, especially not in the winter. We're always saying we should get out of our routine."

Tilly looked at him doubtfully. "Do you mean our routine of not freezing to death?"

"We didn't freeze to death that time. In fact I don't remember feeling the cold at all. It was pretty hot as I recall!" said Elmer.

Tilly gave him a little smile.

•

Elmer had driven out to visit Tilly one Saturday morning after a big snowstorm the night before. It was thrilling to be with Tilly, but he couldn't find much to talk about with his future mother-in-law. He and Tilly had gone all the way a couple of weeks earlier. Since then, every second they weren't together was excruciating. Elmer felt like a real man now, but he could still feel himself blushing whenever Tilly's mom looked at him. He imagined that she knew everything just by looking at his face. He told himself that was impossible, since she and Tilly's dad were probably too old to remember sex at all, but still…

With all the snow, Tilly and her mother were surprised he had made it all the way from town. Wild horses couldn't have kept him away, but the roads were still snowy so Tilly's mother wouldn't let them drive anywhere until the roads were plowed. Elmer had planned to spend the afternoon with Tilly under a pile of blankets in the front seat of his pickup, behind a hedgerow down the road, but that idea was foiled. Tilly and her mom fixed lunch as Elmer tried to come up with an alternate plan.

Lunch was both wonderful and agonizing. Whenever Tilly's mom looked away, Tilly would make a little gesture with her tongue, or wink at him, or make a silent kiss in his direction, or close her eyes and open her mouth as though she was having a silent orgasm. Elmer's erection was throbbing, trapped inside his tight jeans. His testicles hurt, and he could feel a little fluid leaking out the tip of his penis. Sitting at the table hid his problem, but he wasn't sure he could stand up when lunch was over, and he was worried that there would be a wet spot in the front of his pants. It was a long lunch. When Tilly's mom got up to wash the dishes, Tilly reached under the table and touched his thigh. That had nearly caused a very

embarrassing climax to the meal. Tilly smiled and got up to help with the dishes, gently dragging her fingernails across the back of his neck as she walked by. After a few minutes he managed to calm down and get up from the table. It was Tilly who suggested they go for a walk.

•

"No, we didn't freeze to death. You were so hot I'm surprised the snow didn't melt for miles around. I couldn't believe my mom let us go," said Tilly with a grin.

"She didn't suspect a thing," said Elmer.

"Oh, I think she suspected everything. She gave me the birth control talk as soon as you went home. It's a good thing she liked you."

"Oh my god!" said Elmer. "So that's why you

insisted I start using a condom after that."

"She made it pretty clear that I had better not get pregnant before I got married. But, she was smiling when she gave me the talk, probably remembering her younger days."

"Well, I'm not wearing a condom this time! Come on, Girl, get on your winter hiking togs. And don't forget the garter belt!"

"OK, let's go, but you'll have to imagine the garter belt. And, how about we take a blanket or two this time?"

•

They had walked past the barn, then down the edge of the south forty, only holding hands after they had gotten out of sight of the house. They were nearly running when they got to the edge of the woods, stopping for a long kiss, then, knowing the way through the woods, they made their way to a small, sunny clearing near the now frozen creek. They were breathing heavily, giggling, not quite knowing how to proceed. They stood in the clearing for a minute, kissing. This was still new to them. Elmer lay down on his back in the snow and pulled Tilly down on top of him.

They were both wearing several layers of long johns, jeans, heavy tops, sweaters, jackets, two pairs of socks, boots, gloves, hats and scarves. Elmer, in too much of a hurry, slid his hands up under Tilly's jacket, sweater and top. She gave a screech when his snowy gloves touched her bare skin. He quickly took the gloves off, but his clothing covered arms wouldn't fit under her several top layers well enough to reach her bra clasp. With an effort he removed his arms from under her jacket.

Elmer decided to dispense with the preliminaries. He rolled over on top of Tilly, pressing her bare lower back into the snow. She gave a gasp, which he interpreted as an approval of his idea. Elmer unbuttoned her slacks and began to pull them down, exposing more of her bare skin to the snow. Tilly kissed him and told him it would be too cold

to do it that way. They stood up and Tilly led Elmer over to a tree, leaned back against it, and quickly slid her lower clothing down just far enough to give Elmer access to her. She undid Elmer's belt and he felt a thrilling shiver of cold air as Tilly pulled his pants and long johns down around his ankles.

•

Elmer got a couple of blankets from the closet,

grabbed a bottle of brandy from the cabinet just for good measure, and they set out toward the woods.

"I hope you know what you're doing," said Tilly.

They had moved into her parent's old house a few years ago. Now they were following the same path they had fifty years before. They sometimes walked this way in the summer, but it had been years since they had seen it in the winter. The sun was nice, but without leaves, the trees revealed a couple of new houses close enough to see the clearing from their upper floor windows. They found a spot out of view behind a fallen tree, but there was no sun there.

"It will have to do," said Elmer.

They spread out the blankets and lay down next to each other.

"Ouch. There's a branch under me," said Tilly.

In fact, there were many branches and rocks under the only spot Tilly felt was sufficiently out of sight of the neighbors. After some effort they found a way to arrange themselves, but it wasn't exactly cozy. Elmer stood up, unzipped his fly, and lowered his long johns a few inches.

"I guess it's pretty cold out here!" observed Tilly.

Elmer's manhood was the size of a cocktail weenie.

•

Fifty years earlier, the feeling of cold air on his legs and midsection had only made Elmer more aroused as he guided his penis into Tilly. The warmth of her vagina combined with the cold air against his bare butt and legs caused him to ejaculate almost as soon as he was inside her. Elmer was panting, the freezing air stinging his lungs, as the delicious spasms seemed to go on forever. He held Tilly tight, savoring the aftershocks between his legs and the delicious freezing air on his butt. He shivered with the combination of cold and the after effects of his orgasm.

As Elmer began to regain his breath and reluctantly return to planet Earth, he had suddenly realized he was freezing. He could see Tilly was freezing too. She hadn't had anything to warm her up as he had. They hurriedly pulled up their clothes and took care to hide the fact that they had been askew. They were both quiet as they walked back toward the house, Elmer considering how perfect the afternoon had been and how tired he suddenly felt. Tilly was pleased that Elmer was happy with their adventure, but she hadn't gotten her share of the excitement. That night, after she got into bed, she had replayed the afternoon's events in her mind, improving Elmer's performance in her imagination using her pillow as a stand in, which, with a little help from her fingers, brought about the desired result.

•

"What's the matter, big boy?" smiled Tilly. "You don't look quite as ready as you did at eighteen!"

Elmer looked crestfallen.

"I'm ready, but apparently the telegraph wires are down because of the cold. The message doesn't seem to have gone through."

Tilly gave his penis a little kiss. "I think it's cute that way," she said.

"That's nice, but being cute isn't its primary

mission!" grumbled Elmer.

Tilly gave his instrument some more attention, but his butt and legs were freezing and her ministrations, which were usually quite effective, weren't having much influence. Tilly began to shiver from the cold and her bottom hurt from whatever was poking her through the blanket.

"I have an idea, Elmer," she said.

"Does it involve getting warm?"

"Probably more than warm! You know that big, white, down comforter we have in the closet. The one that's so thick and soft?" asked Tilly.

"Yes."

"Let's go back to the house, spread it out in front of the fireplace, and pretend it's snow!"

Elmer gave her a hug. "You're a genius," he said.

Elmer built a fire and they sat on the floor, leaning back against the front of the sofa as they sipped brandy, gradually warmed up, and eased out of their winter clothing. Elmer stood up so Tilly could pull off the last of his layers.

"Hey, it looks like the message has gotten through!" she laughed, giving Elmer a kiss on his belly.

"It sure has!" Elmer observed. "Are you ready for a special delivery?"

~~~
~~~

TILLY'S AFTERNOON DELIGHT

"Oh my goodness!" said Tilly as Elmer came into the living room, "This is just nothing but trash!"

"What's trash?" asked Elmer, not really wanting to know.

"This novel I'm reading on my iPad, *Wanda Wanks the Woodsman.*"

"Who thinks up novels like that?" Elmer asked.

"Apparently thousands of authors with time on their hands, judging by what I find on the internet."

"Why did you pick that one?"

"The cover," said Tilly. "I liked the way he's holding her breast with one hand and his axe handle with the other."

"Why are you reading it if it's trash?"

"I'm not above reading trash. Besides, it's titillating trash. It's about a burly woodsman who rescues an eighteen-year-old virgin who's being held captive in a secret cabin by a rapacious land developer who's about to rape her AND the environment! Now he has to escape with her through the forest."

"Let me guess," said Elmer. "She's so grateful she begs him to deflower her in a bed of maidenhair ferns?"

"You should be a writer!" said Tilly.

"Right. Maybe I'll write about a couple of horny sexagenarians from Iowa," Elmer said with a laugh.

"I'm sure THAT will set the world on fire!"

"Maybe I have hidden talents you know nothing about!" mused Elmer.

"It could be," said Tilly. "But if you do have hidden talents, they've remained well hidden for the fifty years I've known you."

"Well, while you're waiting for them to be revealed, don't forget that Johnson is coming to prune that big oak tree in the back yard this afternoon."

"I can never remember that Johnson kid's first name," said Tilly.

"He and his old man just go by their last name," said Elmer. "That's why you can't remember it. I think the old man's retired now so the kid is running the business these days. Meanwhile, Eddie and I are going to try and beat the heat by going fishing for the afternoon. I'll be back around five-thirty. Don't get so engrossed in your dirty book that you forget to fix dinner."

"I hope he's able to escape," said Tilly, looking down at her iPad.

"That shouldn't be a problem. Meg usually doesn't give Eddie a hard time about going fishing."

"Don't tell me he's going to carry her up into that tree and leave her there!" said Tilly, not looking up.

"Not this time," said Elmer. "Eddie's just going to lock Meg in the crawl space while we're gone."

"Ok, have fun," said Tilly frowning.

•

"The Woodsman picked Wanda up, roughly threw her over his shoulder, pinned her thighs against his bare chest, and, holding his axe in the same hand, scrambled effortlessly up the huge tree. They were soon hidden in the

dense foliage. Wanda's face was pressed against the Woodsman's powerful back as she gasped for breath. The side of the cold steel axe head pressed against the naked, pale skin on the backs of her delicate thighs.

'Take off your shirt and give it to me,' said the Woodsman. Wanda, shaking with fear, did as she was told.

'Now, wait here until I come back!' he said, starting back down the tree."

•

Tilly was startled by a knock at the back door. "Mrs. Talbot?" a shirtless young man called through the screen. "I'm here to work on the oak tree."

Tilly put her tablet down, checked her hair in the mirror, and went to the door. "Hello, Johnson," she said. "It'll be hard, won't it, working in this heat?"

"I'm used to it, Mrs. Talbot," he said, giving her a smile that she found very sexy.

Tilly noticed how the sweat glistened on his muscular chest.

"All right," said Tilly. "I'll come out and sit in the shade in case you want to ask me which limbs need the most attention."

Tilly moved one of the reclining beach chairs into the shade and lowered the back to a forty-five degree angle as Johnson, clad only in cut off shorts and work boots, brought a gaggle of ropes and saws from his truck.

"It's so hot, I'm going to make myself a gin and tonic," Tilly said to Johnson. "Would you like one before you get started?"

"Oh no, Mrs. Talbot. Not now," Johnson said. "Maybe when I'm done climbing." Tilly was convinced he was trying to look down her top when he said it.

"Suit yourself. There's plenty of refreshment available whenever you want it."

Tilly went inside, fixed a tall gin and tonic, and got her iPad. She decided it was too hot to wear a bra all afternoon, so she took hers off and left an extra button undone when she put her shirt back on. When she got back outside, Johnson was already at the top of the tree, attaching a safety rope to an upper branch. His movements in the tree gave her an unusual perspective, looking up at his muscular legs spread across two branches and his buttocks encased in the tight shorts, which were becoming damp with sweat.

•

"After an hour, Wanda heard a noise in the tree below her. Was it an animal, the evil developer, or the Woodsman, back to continue their escape? Looking down, she saw a creature come into view. At first she thought it was a bear, but when she saw the axe, she knew it was the Woodsman.

'We have to go!' he ordered. There was no sign of her shirt.

Again he scrambled down the tree with Wanda over his shoulder and her thighs bound to his chest by his muscular arms. Once on the ground, he took her hand and they began to run back in the direction they had come. The ground was rough and Wanda had a hard time avoiding a fall as the Woodsman, sure footed as a mountain goat, pressed forward at a fast pace."

•

Tilly looked up from her reading, took a sip of her gin and tonic, and checked on Johnson's progress. As she watched, he held his chain saw in one hand while he reached up to a branch above his head with the other and pulled himself up until he could reach out with a foot and gain purchase on a neighboring limb. He had quite a bit of equipment with him as he worked, most of which was attached to the belt of his shorts. This had the effect of causing them to slip down his hips so as to alternately reveal the upper portion of his buttocks or the upper fringe of his pubic area as he swiveled around in the canopy. Tilly took another sip of her gin and tonic, and was surprised to find the glass empty when she finished. She lay back and watched Johnson, seemingly without a care in the world, risking life and limb as he moved gracefully from branch to branch like a wild animal. She closed her eyes for a minute and let the memories of lazy, romantic, delicious summer afternoons, when something exciting was bound to happen, wash over her. Tilly imagined Johnson as a ballet dancer or a gymnast, effortlessly moving his body to present a series of beautiful shapes in the treetop. The air was still, with only an occasional slight breeze to remind her of the stillness. Heat waves rose from the field west of the house. A tickle of sweat trickled down between Tilly's breasts. The areas where her shorts or skin touched the chair were wet with sweat. Insects buzzed in the bed of ferns along the north wall of the garage.

Tilly opened her eyes and watched Johnson work. He was good at his job, and he was equally good at unselfconsciously moving his body into positions that Tilly found wonderfully seductive. In the midst of her reverie, she suddenly realized that another gin and tonic might be a good idea. Tilly unhurriedly got up, peeling her skin from the sticky plastic chair, and went into the kitchen. She mixed another drink, being less careful to limit the amount of gin this time, unbuttoned another button on her shirt, and went back out to the yard. Johnson was on the ground waiting for her.

"Ready for your gin and tonic?" she asked.

"Not yet," he said. "I just need you to look at something."

He put his hand on her lower back and guided her

to a particular vantage point where she could see the part of the canopy where he had been working. She could feel the heat of his hand gently pressing against her back and the cool wet area where their sweat had soaked her shirt as he removed his hand and put it around her shoulder.

"See that big limb there that's cut just this side of the branch going up?" he asked, leaning his face close to hers and pointing so she could align her eye with the tip of his pointing finger.

"Oh, yes."

"Should I cut it back further so that piece of wood pointing up is gone?"

"No, I like seeing that long piece of wood standing up that way."

"Ok, I'm happy to do it any way that pleases you!" he said, heading back to work.

Tilly resumed her reading, watching Johnson out of the corner of her eye as he worked.

•

"As they ran along the rough forest trail, Wanda thought she could hear someone following them from time to time, but all she could do was struggle to keep up with the Woodsman whose strength was undiminished. As they were crossing a small creek, she slipped and would have fallen hard if the Woodsman had not had a tight grip on her hand. As it was, she only twisted her ankle.

'Is your leg OK?' said the Woodsman.

'I think so,' said Wanda, even though it hurt.

Before long, Wanda began to limp, slowing down their pace. The sounds in the distance behind them became louder, and after a time, the Woodsman stopped, put his arm around Wanda's waist and picked her up, holding her under his arm like one would carry a small child who was destined for a spanking. He turned off the trail and made his way through thick brush for some distance until he felt it was safe to stop. A large tree, whose trunk split into two large branches about four feet above the ground, was nearby. The Woodsman gently set Wanda on the ground. Then, placing his hands on her waist, he lifted her up so that she was sitting in the crotch of the tree facing him.

'Give me your bra!' he said to her.

She removed the only remaining garment above her waist and gave it to him, covering her naked bosom as well as she could with her hand. He moved his body between her outstretched legs, then gently began to wrap her injured ankle with the bra, stretching the elastic to make a tight wrap.

Their run through the brush had caused a cut on Wanda's thigh, which was now beginning to bleed. The Woodsman lifted Wanda down from her seat in the tree and stood her in front of him. Without a word, he undid the fasteners on the front of her torn shorts and pulled them, along with her panties, down to her ankles, taking her legs one at a time and lifting them out of the last of her clothing. She was completely naked."

•

Tilly took a long drink of her gin and tonic. She looked up at Johnson, whose wet shorts clung to his otherwise nearly naked body. As he looked down at her and smiled, she noticed that he appeared to have an erection, which, she observed, was about the only thing keeping his shorts from slipping down to his ankles given the slipperiness of his body and the heavy equipment he carried. Tilly wondered if he had a girlfriend. She took another long drink and closed her eyes for a second, picturing what would happen to Johnson's shorts if the top button were to become undone.

•

"The Woodsman knelt in front of Wanda, his breath tickling the back of Wanda's hand as she tried to cover her virginal pubic area. He picked up her torn panties, rubbed them with a medicinal herb that he took from his pocket, and carefully wrapped them around her thigh, covering the cut and stopping the bleeding. 'Thank you,' she said.

The Woodsman looked up at her childlike face. 'You're a pretty girl,' he smiled.

Wanda stood up carefully and tested her ankle. She felt she could walk a little way at least, and, forgetting she was naked, took the Woodsman's hand and led him to a nearby bed of maidenhair ferns. Kneeling in front of him, she removed his rough trousers, then lay back, motioning for him to lie on top of her."

Johnson had now finished with his work and stood looking down at Tilly. "What do you think?"

Tilly looked up at his body, which was nearly naked and looked huge against the sky from her perspective.

"Awesome!" she said, using a word she didn't ever remember uttering before, but which she assumed would be understood by the young man in front of her. "Are you ready for that gin and tonic?"

"You bet!" he said, pulling a lawn chair up next to her beach chair, which she began to think of as more of a bed than a chair.

"Could you get it sweetheart?" Tilly asked. "The fixings are on the counter in the kitchen."

"Sure!" said Johnson. "Do you want another one?"

"I want a big stiff one," said Tilly, starting to giggle after she realized how that had come out.

He brought the drinks and they talked about his

work and how exciting it must be to climb trees for a living. Tilly revealed that she was an expert tree climber as a kid, but hadn't tried it for years.

"There's really nothing to it," said Johnson. "You could climb that tree as well as me with a little help."

"No I couldn't!" said Tilly, taking a sip of her third gin and tonic and reacting with surprise at how strong Johnson had made them.

"Come on!" he said, standing up and taking her hand.

"Really?" she said. He pulled her up to her feet.

"Sure. I'll show you how it's done!"

He helped her to the base of the tree, turned her to face him, and lifted her by the waist on to a large branch about four feet above the ground.

"There you go, you did it," he said.

Even though there was no breeze, the tree seemed to be swaying.

"I don't know how I'm going to get down now!" Tilly said, without a shred of concern.

"Don't worry, I'll be gentle with you," said Johnson.

He reached up, put his strong hands on her waist and slid her off the branch toward him. Tilly was a little off balance and put her foot out in front of her as he did so, catching her toes in the waistband of his shorts and pushing them down to his ankles as he lowered her into his arms. Tilly looked down and discovered he wasn't wearing any underwear.

"Well, Mrs. Talbot, that certainly opens up some new possibilities!" he said, as he gave her a soft, delicious kiss.

He kicked off his shorts, and, wearing only his boots, carried her back to the beach chair where he laid her gently onto her back.

Again he was towering over her, his erection looking like one of the branches of the oak tree behind him.

"It's so big!" she said, dreamily.

A hand touched her inner thigh.

"What's so big?" said Elmer, leaning over her.

"Johnson's...," said Tilly, squinting as she looked up.

"Johnson's what, his bill for the tree?"

"Johnson, um, I mean Johnson's...," she stared at the blurry figure above her. "Elmer?" she said.

"Of course. Was the bill too high do you think? How much was it?"

"Oh, no, not the bill. I don't think he even gave me a bill. Where did he go?"

"He's been gone a while, I guess. I passed his truck on the way out from town. What was so big?"

"Oh, nothing," said Tilly.

"Elmer?"

"What?"

"Have we ever made love in a bed of maidenhair ferns?"

<div align="center">~~~</div>

ABOUT THE AUTHOR

Gene Clements is an author and artist in Berkeley, California. He has drawn the figure for four decades and his drawings have been exhibited in group shows throughout the Bay Area and at the Seattle Erotic Art Festival. Like Tilly and Elmer, he imagines himself to be eighteen, even though he has not been eighteen for a half century.

Gene grew up in a small town in central Illinois. His mother was an artist and his father an English teacher; no doubt both would be shocked to learn that Gene eventually began to follow in their footsteps, and even more shocked at the content of his efforts. He earned degrees in architecture from the University of Illinois and MIT and practiced architecture and taught architectural history and computer-aided design for many years before turning his focus primarily toward drawing and writing. Gene drew the cover and illustrations for this book on an iPad using the Artstudio app.

TILLY AND ELMER TITLES

Collections and individual story titles in the Tilly and Elmer Series, formatted for your favorite e-reader, are available in the Amazon Kindle Store, the Apple iBook Store, Barnes and Noble Nook Store, and at Smashwords, Kobo, Sony, and others.

A companion series, ***Coming of Age in South Branch***, is a complete collection of stories in the Tilly and Elmer FlashbackX series, an account of the do-it-yourself sex education of the nineteen-sixties. In this sweet, nostalgic, funny, (and sometimes dirty) book, Tilly and Elmer remember their romantic and awkward high school dating years, from their first date, in 1961, through the night they finally went "all the way", to their heart-wrenching departures for distant colleges in 1963. You may find these stories sounding a little familiar as Tilly and Elmer reveal the clumsy interactions, the shocking miscommunication, and the catastrophes that seem funny in retrospect, as well as the surprising delights and breathtaking pleasures of learning about sex and falling hopelessly in love.

You can find links to any of these individual titles and collections, as well as more drawings and info, at TillyandElmer.com.